Nip it! Dig it!

Written by Natasha Paul

Collins

Tig nips at it.

Sid digs a pit.

Sid

a pit

dig

5

Tad naps on Tom.

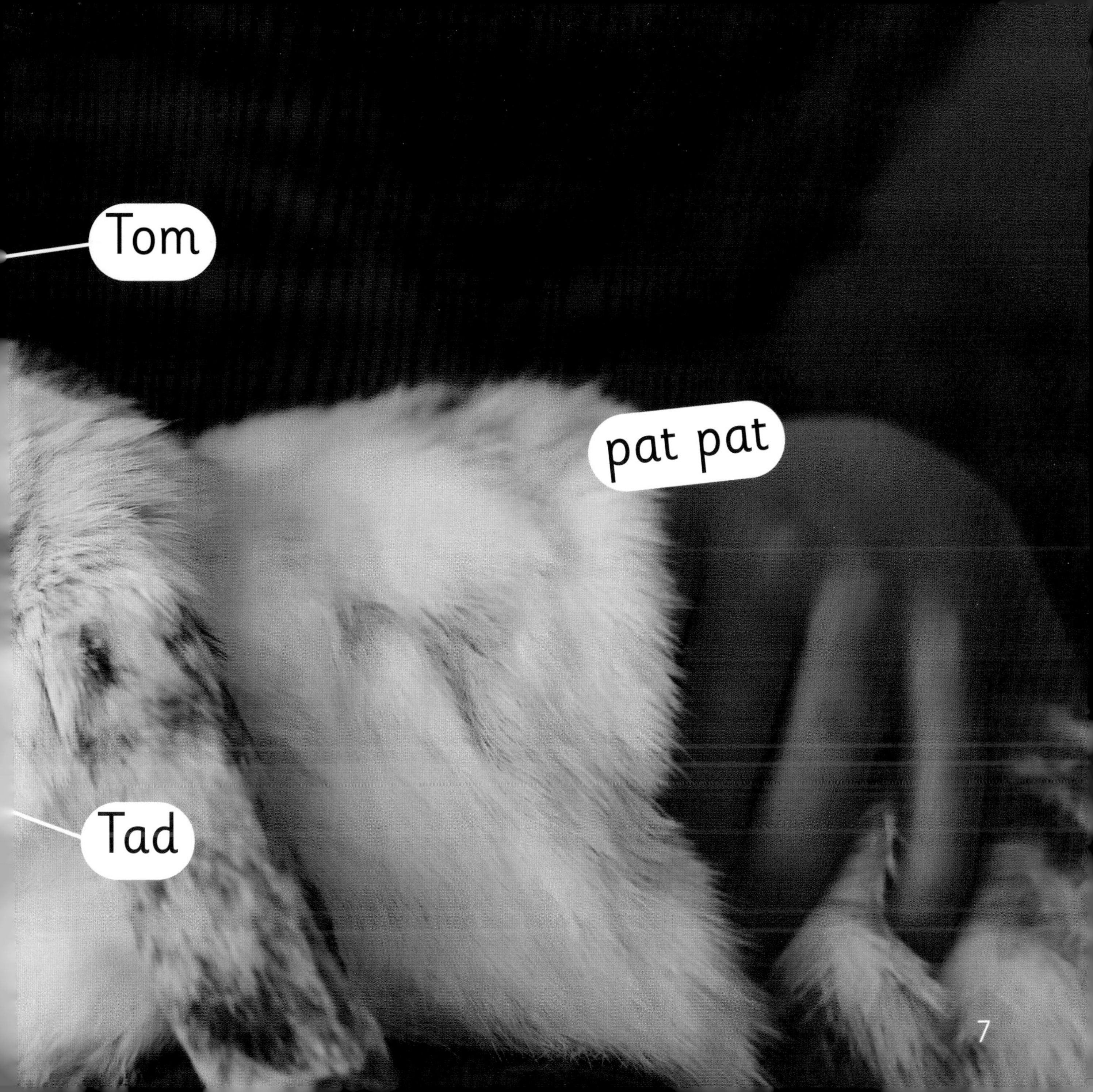
Tom
pat pat
Tad

Tog sits. Tog sips.

Tog

a pot

dots

9

Pip sits on top.

Pip nips a pod.

Pog naps in it.

Nap in a pot!

/o/

14

 After reading

Letters and Sounds: Phase 2

Word count: 48

Focus phonemes: /g/ /o/

Curriculum links: Understanding the world

Early learning goals: Reading: read and understand simple sentences; use phonic knowledge to decode regular words and read them aloud accurately

Developing fluency

- Your child may enjoy hearing you read the book.
- You could each choose to read the main text or the labels. You could swap from page 8.

Phonic practice

- Turn to page 2. Ask your child to sound out the letters in the word **nips**. (n/i/p/s – **nips**) Check they don't miss the last **s**.
- On pages 4–5, focus on the words **Sid**, **digs** and **pit**. Ask your child to sound out and blend each word, checking they don't muddle the end sound.
- Look at the "I spy sounds" pages (14–15). Point to the log and say: I spy an /o/ in log. Challenge your child to point to and name different things they can see containing the /o/ sound. (e.g. *pod, pot, box, dots, Tog, orange, tomatoes, hopping, rocks*)

Extending vocabulary

- Turn to page 3 and discuss the meaning of **gap**. Ask your child what other words could be used instead. (e.g. *hole, space*) Can they see a gap anywhere in their room now?
- On page 6, discuss the meaning of **naps**. Ask your child what other words could be used instead. (e.g. *snoozes, sleeps, dozes*) Ask them to read the sentence with their suggested word to make sure it makes sense.